THE

LITTLE

WOMAN

WANTED

NOISE

THIS IS A NEW YORK REVIEW BOOK
PUBLISHED BY THE NEW YORK REVIEW OF BOOKS
435 Hudson Street, New York, NY 10014
www.nyrb.com

Library of Congress Cataloging-in-Publication Data
Teal, Val.
The little woman wanted noise / by Val Teal ; illustrated by Robert
Lawson.
    pages cm. — (New York Review books children's collection)
First published in Chicago by Rand McNally & Company in 1943.
Summary: The Little Woman loves living in the big city despite all of
the noise, so when she is given a peaceful farm in the country and finds it
too quiet to be relaxing, she sets out to make it feel like home.
ISBN 978-1-59017-711-2 (hardback)
[1. Noise—Fiction. 2. Farm life—Fiction. 3. Domestic animals—Fiction.
4. Animal sounds—Fiction. 5. Adoption—Fiction.] I. Lawson, Robert,
1892-1957, illustrator. II. Title.
PZ7.T22Li 2013
[E]—dc23
                                                    2013018763

ISBN 978-1-59017-711-2

Cover design by Louise Fili Ltd.

Printed in the United States on acid-free paper.
1 3 5 7 9 10 8 6 4 2

THE
LITTLE WOMAN WANTED
NOISE

By Val Teal

Pictures by Robert Lawson

THE NEW YORK REVIEW CHILDREN'S COLLECTION
New York

To John, Peter, and Topper

whose noise inspires

the little woman

ONCE there was a little woman who lived in a big city. She had lived there all her life.

Motorbuses bumped by her door. Big trucks loaded with lumber and bricks rattled down her street. All day long people hurried past her window—newsboys yelling, children running and screaming, men shouting, women *tap-tap tapping* along on their clattery high heels.

On one side of the little woman lived a shoemaker. All day long the shoemaker made merry noises with his hammer and his sewing machine.

On the other side of the little woman lived a carpenter. All day long the carpenter made merry noises with his hammer and saw.

Upstairs in the little woman's house lived a printer. All day long the printer made a merry noise with his big printing press.

One day the little woman got a letter. It was from her cousin in the country. It said, "I am going to Australia and I give you my farm."

"That will be a nice place for me to live," said the little woman to herself. "I will sell my house and move to the pleasant, peaceful farm."

So she did.

The farm was green and pretty. There were meadows and fields and an apple orchard and a brook. And there was a big red barn and a little white farmhouse with a wide porch. The farmhouse was clean and comfortable, and the little woman liked it.

But she couldn't rest and she had no peace of mind because it was so quiet.

So she walked half a mile to her nearest neighbor and she said, "What can I do to get some noise on my place?"

And the neighbor said, "Why, buy some animals, to be sure. Buy some animals, by all means. Animals with voices to them."

"Thank you," said the little woman.

And she hurried away and bought a cow.

Moo-moo, said the cow, and the little woman thought that was a fine noise.

But it was not enough.

"I must get more noises on my farm," she said.

So she bought a dog.

Bow-wow, said the dog, and the little woman thought that was a fine noise.

Now, all day long, she could hear *bow-wow* . . . *moo-moo* . . . *bow-wow.* She liked it, but it was not enough, and she had no rest or peace of mind.

So she bought a cat.

RL

Meow-meow, said the cat, and the little woman thought that was a fine noise.

Now the noises on the farm went *meow-meow* . . . *bow-wow* . . . *moo-moo* . . . *meow-meow*. But still the little woman wanted more.

So she bought a duck.

Quack-quack, said the duck, and the little woman thought that was a fine noise.

So now she had these noises: *quack-quack . . . meow-meow . . . bow-wow . . . moo-moo . . . quack-quack.* But still the farm was too quiet for the little woman.

So she bought a hen and a rooster.

Cut-cut-cut—cut-aw-cut, said the hen, and the rooster said *cock-a-doodle-doo.* The little woman thought those were fine noises.

And the hen sat on some eggs and hatched them into little chicks. And the little chicks ran all over the yard, saying *peep-peep—peep-peep.*

So now, most of the day, the little woman could hear *peep-peep* . . . *cock-a-doodle-doo* . . . *cut-cut-cut—cut-aw-cut* . . . *quack-quack* . . . *meow-meow* . . . *bow-wow* . . . *moo-moo* . . . *peep-peep—peep-peep*.

The little woman liked it, but still it was not enough, and she had no rest or peace of mind.

So she bought a pig.

And every once in a while the pig made a grand long noise like this: *sque-ee-ee-e-e-e.* It sounded good with the *peep-peep . . . cock-a-doodle-doo . . . cut-cut-cut—cut-aw-cut . . . quack-quack . . . meow-meow . . . bow-wow . . . moo-moo.*

But the little woman wanted even more noise on her farm.

So she bought an old rattlety-bang car with a good loud horn.

Goo-oo-oop, said the horn. *Goo-oo-oop.*

So whenever it was too quiet, the little woman sat in the old rattlety-bang car and honked the horn.

Then the animals would all start up, and there would be a grand large noise like this: *Goop-oo-oop . . . sque-ee-e . . . peep-peep . . . cock-a-doodle-doo . . . cut-aw-cut . . . quack-quack . . . meow-meow . . . bow-wow . . . moo-moo . . . goo-oo-oop.*

But still it was not enough for the little woman.

So one day she got into her old rattlety-bang car and drove off to the big city.

She drove up one street and down another until she came to a place where she heard the most terrific noise. She stopped the car and listened. It was lovely.

So the little woman got out and went in. The place was full of BOYS. Big boys . . . little boys . . . thin boys . . . fat boys . . . boys with curly black hair . . . boys with straight yellow hair . . . boys with standing-up red hair. And all of them were noisy.

But a big boy with curly dark hair and a little boy with standing-up red hair were the noisiest of them all. And when they were noisy together they were ten times noisier than when they were noisy apart.

The little woman said, "This noise . . . is . . . DELICIOUS."

And she took the big boy with curly dark hair and the little boy with standing-up red hair home with her.

After that, there was always plenty of noise on the farm.

It was NEVER quiet.

And the little woman had no rest.
But she had peace of mind.

VAL TEAL (1902–1997) was born in Bottineau, North Dakota, on February 14th, the third generation in her family to be born on Valentine's Day. She did undergraduate work at the University of Minnesota during the 1920s and worked for many years as a tutor in the humanities at the University of Nebraska, Omaha. From the 1930s on she contributed personal essays and stories to such magazines as *Saturday Evening Post*, *Woman's Home Companion*, *Ladies' Home Journal*, *Good Housekeeping*, and *Parents*, but it was not until 1943 that she published her first book, *The Little Woman Wanted Noise*. In addition to her stories for children, Teal also wrote a memoir of motherhood, *It Was Not What I Expected*.

ROBERT LAWSON (1892–1957) was a prolific writer and illustrator of literature for children and was the first person ever to receive both the Newbery and Caldecott medals. Among his forty-odd books are such classic stories as *Rabbit Hill*, *Ben and Me*, and *They Were Strong and Good*. In addition to *The Little Woman Wanted Noise*, The New York Review Children's Collection publishes *Wee Gillis* by Munro Leaf, with illustrations by Robert Lawson.

TITLES IN
THE NEW YORK REVIEW CHILDREN'S COLLECTION

ESTHER AVERILL
Captains of the City Streets
The Hotel Cat
Jenny and the Cat Club
Jenny Goes to Sea
Jenny's Birthday Book
Jenny's Moonlight Adventure
The School for Cats

JAMES CLOYD BOWMAN
Pecos Bill: The Greatest Cowboy of All Time

PALMER BROWN
Beyond the Pawpaw Trees
Cheerful
Hickory
The Silver Nutmeg
Something for Christmas

SHEILA BURNFORD
Bel Ria: Dog of War

DINO BUZZATI
The Bears' Famous Invasion of Sicily

CARLO COLLODI and FULVIO TESTA
Pinocchio

INGRI and EDGAR PARIN D'AULAIRE
D'Aulaires' Book of Animals
D'Aulaires' Book of Norse Myths
D'Aulaires' Book of Trolls
Foxie: The Singing Dog
The Terrible Troll-Bird
Too Big
The Two Cars

EILÍS DILLON
The Island of Horses
The Lost Island

ELEANOR FARJEON
The Little Bookroom

PENELOPE FARMER
Charlotte Sometimes

PAUL GALLICO
The Abandoned

RUMER GODDEN
An Episode of Sparrows
The Mousewife

LUCRETIA P. HALE
The Peterkin Papers

RUSSELL and LILLIAN HOBAN
The Sorely Trying Day

RUTH KRAUSS and MARC SIMONT
The Backward Day

DOROTHY KUNHARDT
Junket Is Nice
Now Open the Box

MUNRO LEAF and ROBERT LAWSON
Wee Gillis

RHODA LEVINE and EDWARD GOREY
Three Ladies Beside the Sea
He Was There from the Day We Moved In

BETTY JEAN LIFTON and EIKOH-HOSOE
Taka-chan and I

NORMAN LINDSAY
The Magic Pudding

ERIC LINKLATER
The Wind on the Moon

J. P. MARTIN
Uncle
Uncle Cleans Up

JOHN MASEFIELD
The Box of Delights
The Midnight Folk

WILLIAM McCLEERY and WARREN CHAPPELL
Wolf Story

E. NESBIT
The House of Arden

DANIEL PINKWATER
Lizard Music

ALASTAIR REID and BOB GILL
Supposing…

ALASTAIR REID and BEN SHAHN
Ounce Dice Trice

BARBARA SLEIGH
Carbonel and Calidor
Carbonel: The King of the Cats
The Kingdom of Carbonel

E. C. SPYKMAN
Terrible, Horrible Edie

FRANK TASHLIN
The Bear That Wasn't

JAMES THURBER
The 13 Clocks
The Wonderful O

ALISON UTTLEY
A Traveller in Time

T. H. WHITE
Mistress Masham's Repose

MARJORIE WINSLOW and ERIK BLEGVAD
Mud Pies and Other Recipes

REINER ZIMNIK
The Bear and the People